Philippe Vasset heads the i
Energy Intelligence, based in F
detective in the US before b
1993, won the prize for Best
French daily *Le Monde*. *ScriptGenerator* is his first novel.

ScriptGenerator
Machines I

Philippe Vasset

Translated by
Jane Metter

Library of Congress Catalog Card Number: 2004103041

A complete catalogue record for this book can
be obtained from the British Library on request

First published in France by Librairie Arthème Fayard, 2003

First published in this English language edition in 2004 by
Serpent's Tail, 4 Blackstock Mews, London N4 2BT
website: www.serpentstail.com

Designed and typeset at Neuadd Bwll, Llanwrtyd Wells
Printed by ChromoLitho in Italy

10 9 8 7 6 5 4 3 2 1

With the support of the
Culture 2000 programme
of the European Union

Education and Culture

Culture 2000

Compelled to please readers from all walks of life rather than shock anyone, we wondered whether a literary work existed which could serve as an example and not as a model. We think we have found it in Dumas' *The Three Musketeers.*

Marcel Allain

(Co-author, with others, of thirty-two episodes of *Fantômas*), 'The popular novel and its commercial possibilities', *Europe*, nos 590–591.

Diamond

I have been meticulously analysing what lies beneath the surface for the last few months, before the others dig beneath the soil to lay down the galleries. The atmosphere is close; dust and insects fill the air.

Above the mine's crater, shafts of sunlight mingle amongst the trees, creating a luminous network which emanates from the clouds of dust, a shimmering spectre of the tunnels which extend beneath the Central African jungle.

I am not the engineer responsible for this operation, far from it. I merely pieced together a geological map from samples recovered from the site. That was what I was employed to do. I was asked very few questions, and I, in turn, scaled down my requirements considerably. I am housed on site, in the sheet-metal shack in which I work. I never voice my opinion on the running of the works, and limit all contact with the mine's managers as much as possible. I am no more sociable with the workers, whose language I don't even speak. I live the way I lived in prison; my one luxury is to sleep outside whenever it is not raining. My discretion is appreciated in this world obsessed with secrecy, and more than once they have alluded to other opportunities which would come my way. I don't have much choice; there is no work for me.

The comings and goings of the machines, the explosions and the subsidence produce constant dust. We live enveloped in the folds of a sheet of dried powder, in an intermediary world between air and matter. Fear of suffocation is ever present, both above and beneath the soil. The red cloud which hovers above the site can thicken at any moment, and bury us alive. Dispersed by the slightest wind, the dust is transformed into mud whenever it rains. It then dries in the sun. With each shower, the mud level rises. My shack, originally positioned on dry land, now rests in a bed of mud, sometimes hard, sometimes malleable. After the rain, small mounds, formed by whatever objects the soil has covered over, litter the site. The following day, we use a pickaxe to break down these heaps in order to recover whatever was taken, possessions which have become relics. If one does not act immediately, the next storm will submerge them further into the soil. Every inch of this terrain is significant, whether it harbours gems compressed millions of years ago or geological relief of the night before last. Little by little we become fossilised.

I was dismantling one of these mounds when I came across my predecessor's possessions. A variety of tales was told about this heap. It was sometimes referred to in hushed tones as the mausoleum in which three workmen were caught stealing stones. No one wanted anything to do with it.

On a rare occasion when I had some free time, I gathered together a fine collection of debris disfigured by the humidity and the earth; these objects were not fine merely because of the exotic materials they were made of but also because of the events they conjured up. I was too curious to be impervious to what might lie hidden beneath this ossified evidence.

Only two cardboard boxes lay hidden beneath the soil; they were squashed and contained exercise books, magazines and some clothing. No one knew what had happened to the owner. He had been recruited in Guinea, had just completed a research project on metal deposits on Mount Nimbi, and wanted to stay in the area. He had worked in Sierra Leone for a while before the civil war intervened, forcing the company to abandon the mines in the region to the rebellion, and concentrate on other licences they held in central Africa. He must have been Swiss or Belgian and his name was Jean.

Inevitably, this vague image would soon become blurred. In Guinea, he was employed by Mano Iron, who knew him as a Canadian called Pierre. The people who employed him had left the company and so the trail ended there. There was no evidence of his stay in Bangui on any immigration list. The only address for him was a box number in Monrovia, a town which was also his financial residence.

In one of the boxes, there is a plastic folder. It contains a piece of paper printed on both sides, carefully detached from what must have been a slim manual. The paper is thick, laminated and wrinkled with creases. No illustrations; just a few black dashes, dots and indents for paragraphs which structure the content. The background is a watery green colour, through which looms a blurred photograph of some tropical undergrowth. The text is perfectly legible.

'Everything has been said.' It's time that you, entrepreneurs, use this mantra of artistic circles to your advantage. If everything has been written, filmed, and acted, if the flow of stories has effectively come to an end, it means **that narrative has finally become raw material, a commodity. Therefore, its treatment can be mechanised**. This manual will demonstrate how this can be done.

Initially in possession of one or two media, you now own several:

- newspapers,
- publishing houses,
- film studios,
- television channels,
- sports teams.

Consequently, **you are subjected to increasing numbers of constraints in an increasingly competitive environment**. You should be launching content which can be exploited in several, if not in every one of your subsidiary companies.

To be profitable, a book, article or comic strip must have the potential to be rapidly converted into a screenplay, a video game or a television programme, which in turn would also be interchangeable: the ideal situation would be if all three could run in tandem. Each product is then submitted to a treatment made up of episodes, which can be rotated pretty quickly: sequel, series, foldback, revenge. Merchandising of course would form part of the process and would include models, clothing, gadgets, etc.

You already know all this; this is bread and butter to you. You also know, faced with an increasingly vast and sophisticated market, that current **production units operate on an outdated model. The human factor is overvalued**, economies of scale are non-existent, and more often than not costs cannot be compressed.

This for one reason only: the production line lacks continuity. Content is still manufactured in two distinctive stages: first, that which is generally referred to as the 'creation', the realm of the 'artist', and, second, the process of manipulating the content (manufacturing, marketing and distribution), which is your group's forte. The tool presented in this manual has been designed to put an end to this anachronism and, to introduce a completely integrated industrial process, one in which the conceptualisation of the product is but one stage in the mechanised manufacturing process. It is ridiculous to allocate millions of dollars to the 'creation' when this part of the production process can be replaced beneficially by a judicious and systematic recycling of two thousand years of narratives, maturing in libraries, archives, data bases.

It is time to exploit rather than succumb to this accumulation of material, which makes the creators, whom you pay so dearly, giddy.

This is the purpose of our presentation. The tool we describe, **the software ScriptGenerator©®™, allows the user to exploit all narrative stock rationally and generate a competitive product, which meets the needs of the market.**

ScriptGenerator©®™ is revolutionary in that it obliterates the 'creative' process, or more specifically, it transforms the production of content into one long treatment of raw material.

This new tool will finally strip the entertainment industry of its unique status; it is the only industry which still develops a product from nothing, ultimately it will be transformed into a genuine industry, one which transforms commodities.

It is the story, the narrative already mature, which is the raw material, and not language.

ScriptGenerator©®™ has not been thought up by artists, not even by 'members of the Profession'. We are simply entrepreneurs, graduates of the commodities market, the most ruthless school in existence. Two of us were originally petroleum engineers. Three others have worked on the Chicago Exchange and another on the London Metal Exchange. As for the Chairman of our Board, he started out as a geologist before pursuing his career in cocoa futures.

The foam spreads across the shore. Like a punch-drunk boxer, the sea ebbs and flows, breaking down as it encounters land.

I wait for the driver who is supposed to drive me to Buchanan, in the far east of Liberia.

The instant I came across the fragment of the prospectus, I left the mine in search of the owner, or at least in search of one of his partners. My reasoning is as follows: I had read a description of a device which, regardless of whether it is up and running or simply being developed, can only function in total secrecy. If the existence of this machine were to come to light, its commercial viability would immediately disappear: who would purchase automatically generated productions? If I were to threaten to reveal the existence of this tool, surely I would be able to obtain significant financial compensation, which would end the need for six-month freelance stints in the desert or the bush.

The trail led me to Monrovia where I consulted bank registers, which, theoretically, are confidential, but in fact accessible to those who are careful enough to leave Central Africa with enough diamonds in a packet of cigarettes to call in favours. The account in my predecessor's name was also used by a forestry business. I set off for the east to meet the manager of this company.

Buchanan Harbour is an offshore enclave in a country which itself is a vast free zone. Even during ten years of civil war, haphazard breakwaters were crumbling beneath the piles of rough timber waiting to be loaded on to the Thai or Malay cargo ships. Today, the fact that the amount demanded at the checkpoints has tripled is the most visible outcome of peace. I only stay in Buchanan a few hours, enough time to find a collective taxi, willing to take me into the forest further north. Later on I fall asleep on the back seat of a van, against a background of what appears to be tree tops overhead swaying on either side of the road, like the graceful dance of an octopus.

Forestry licences here seem to be exploited against all better judgement. Whereas others take care to chop down only mature and valuable trees like the Niangon, Framine, Sipo, Iroko, Ekki and Abura, here nothing has been spared. Tree trunks too old to be sold are piled up, boles of thin trees carefully sawed, even stumps. Over dozens of hectares nothing is left: all the trees have been cut low, to soil level. No camps, no slash-and-burn farming. Only arborescence of sawdust and dried-out wood on the red soil. Trucks clearly don't often pass through here.

After a few hours, a man bent over taking photographs of the soil. My driver has left me a long time ago, as the road progressively disappeared. I go nearer; I am looking for the manager of this operation. Dead silence. He barely raises his head. I carry on talking; calmly he pulls out a gun, loads it and places it next to him. I sit down and say nothing. He takes out a large sheet of paper from his bag and places it on the tree stump he has just photographed. He draws, using a piece of charcoal, with a light hand and regular strokes. The wood's concentric circles are clearly visible on the grey outline which materialises after an hour. A piece of tracing paper is then placed on top of the same tree stump and the same circles are carefully traced over with a pencil. Once he has put the pieces of paper away he invites me to follow him.

The site barracks are completely deserted. With my guide, I go in to a sheet-metal cabin whose door is heavily padlocked. Once I have sat down, I have to explain myself. The walls are covered with topographical and geological maps, some of which are quite old, and photographs and drawings of tree trunks. Some of the vein irregularities in the wood are circled in red. Some of the tree stumps' tracings are piled up and positioned against a lightbulb, highlighting the differences between the concentric circles. I explain I am looking for an old friend who must have worked on this project quite recently. He is a French-speaking engineer, who had access to your company's bank account. Of course, but he has never worked here. He sits on the board of a company of which this project is only a subsidiary. I have only seen him once myself. Why are you looking for him? I have a document for him; what is the name of your holding company? Executive Associates, a Liberian-registered shipping firm, based in London. To fill up their ships they are also involved in wood, cocoa and rubber. Does my friend come here often? Never. I hold a rather unusual position in the organisation: I am a majority shareholder in this project, but this project is not meant to be profitable. It is a reward for services rendered.

Some time later, a clerk working in what serves as the Buchanan Harbour office gives me the full run down on the story. But when I woke up the following day, I was alone. I returned to the harbour in a mini-bus, jam-packed with a mixture of passengers and goods; so chaotic that it was impossible to identify all the different elements. Nearly a week has passed since then, and during that time I have been hanging around the docks searching for a cargo ship to take me to London. Over a beer, I discover that the man photographing tree trunks was once an undersecretary for maritime trade in the Liberian government. In exchange for helping a group of western investors set up companies, he received a forestry concession where he lives in exile. He belongs to an ethnic group which was virtually decimated during the war; he has spent years trying to piece together his tribe's history. The only archives he possesses are the line drawings of the light brown circles which feature on the tree pulp. Sometimes he sells a few steres of wood to subsist, but most of the bark is left in situ, cut into round slices, labelled and classified. He has, apparently, started to write a book.

As for me, I am still trying to decipher the whole thing. I take a job in the harbour office whilst waiting for a cargo ship. My work entails logging the ships as they berth and depart. I inspect the quays, I make a note of the captains' intentions and then my employer, in a few words, lodges the information in a large book. As in the forest, a book is being written in Buchanan. For reasons of confidentiality, all maritime traffic is recorded in code, based on a complex system of equivalences. Two letters corresponds to each piece of information, registration details, transported merchandise, owner and insurer's names, date of arrival and departure. Words are then made up from these binomials, which are subsequently inscribed in the logbook kept in the harbour office. There is no punctuation. The order never changes: owner, nature and origin of cargo, destination and crew nationality. The long text this information conjures up is largely unintelligible, but the employees know entire pages, which include some very old entries, by heart. On the jetty, children recite the entries as they play. Using the same code, the labourers use chalk to mark the containers with cryptograms to identify the contents. In the bars, clients are described to the girls in mysterious terms. And the crews, oblivious to everything, circulate amongst this crowd who can see right through them.

I learn the code. Initially, so that I can read the inscriptions written on the containers lining the docks. Bundles of used clothing (UC) for Sierra Leone (SL), copper boxes (CO) from Zambia (ZA), bags of coffee (CF) from Jinja (Uganda UG) destined for Burma (MY), generators (GE), sacks of rice (RZ) forming long subordinate clauses from various countries of origin (CI, ML, ID), punctuated with barrels of Brent crude (BR) and bitumen (BM). And also because learning this idiom will help me find a ship. One day, I see EXHUME RUBBLE scribbled on a bag of food being carried by a cargo ship chef to the market. EXHUME RUBBLE translates as: the man carrying the bag is one of the crew on a ship belonging to Executive Associates (EX) which is transporting coal (HU) from Mauritania (ME) destined for the United Kingdom (RU), with a crew from Barbados (BB), once it has unloaded its cargo of electrical cables (LE). I follow the sailor to his ship, an enormous, ageing wreck registered in Riga. I discover he is leaving the day after tomorrow. I must get on board, I need to get back to London, but more importantly the man I am looking for also works for Executive Associates.

I did not find out anything during the crossing. The journey proves to be a long series of photographic clichés frozen by the ship's indecisive rolling between two waves, a sleepy drifting from one image to the next. The captain gives me a discount on the cost of the crossing in exchange for my ability to read maritime maps. But regular consultations with the map do not dispel my feeling of loss. I am reeling.

I disembark at Felixstowe, the United Kingdom's second container port, and wait for the captain behind a boathouse. When he finally emerges at sundown, I follow him along the docks. I am not the only person to be following him: a woman dressed in grey advances cautiously between the two of us. Our trio's progression is both swift and indecisive, accentuated by flamboyant shadows. Suddenly the woman slips and falls. The captain scans the darkness to see if he can work out where the noise is coming from, then runs off. I also start to run; I reach the woman, who gets up with difficulty. She has dropped her bag and it lies open on the drenched soil. Amongst the sheets of paper which are absorbing the water, I see, enclosed in a plastic folder, a more legible sheet. I grab it and run as fast as I can through the deserted harbour.

Later, I carefully empty the contents of the folder onto my hotel room bed. The first page, a watery light-green-coloured sheet of laminated paper, is identical to the one in my possession, possibly in better condition. The layout of the second page is also identical, but the text is different.

1 A commodities trader's greatest asset is a virtually encyclopaedic knowledge of all properties pertaining to the materials bought and sold, as well as a subtle understanding of his consumers' needs. A good diamond dealer, for example, would trade not only with jewellers, but also with the optics and electronics industries. (Traditionally, diamonds have always been considered precious, but they are also very hard stones, i.e., capable of engraving and cutting through indestructible alloy. They are also extremely pure, which means they can refract the most complex lights.) Similarly, gold is traded both for its rarity, which confers upon it a speculative value, and for its malleability: gold can be stretched out at will.

ScriptGenerator©®™ has been designed to be a good trader in stories. Over and above being a piece of equipment which will generate intrigue, it is first and foremost an intermediary which identifies your needs, and offers you a variety of suitable materials. These materials are the structures, characters and events which feature in all novels, TV series, films, musical comedies and video games ever printed, as well as all historical events both major and minor (which not only include the timeline of the story and its key players, but also the costumes, tools, décor and any additional details which serve to amplify the narrative).

2 To understand how **ScriptGenerator©®™** overturns the production process by making us see the final content, the 'work of art' as product, we must return to raw materials.

To maintain profit margins in the highly competitive metal, petrol and agricultural commodity market, traders need to duck and dive. During the 1990s some of us perfected the most elaborate cost-cutting strategies in order to satisfy our clients. Marketing trash goods was one strategy: virtually dry petrol wells, virtually worn-out mines, degraded stocks. Bought for a pittance, all these assets still conceal some resources, which are inaccessible to large corporations but accessible if primitive techniques are used. These include manual exploitation of a mine's narrow galleries, which cannot accommodate heavy machinery, using inordinately large mini-derricks instead of cumbersome platforms, converting salvaged pharmaceutical waste into glucose syrup, recycling animal carcasses and rejects into flour etc.

ScriptGenerator©®™ applies these avant-garde techniques which have proved themselves on both the London and Chicago Stock Exchanges, to the narrative market. Using low-cost techniques, **ScriptGenerator®©™** fills in storylines with recycled narrative twists.

3 This new industrial process has already revolutionized the music industry: CD production today is a systematic engineering of already existing sounds which are reprocessed or remixed. Initially, sampling, the process which creates something out of quotations (a bass line from a piece of music, a line from a song, etc) from other works, was used by only a few artists who were convinced that the use of repetition in the re-edit, was, in itself, an act of creation in a saturated cultural market.

The music industry was quick to spot the economic advantages of such a process – using existing components in production keeps costs down and also reduces the amount spent on salaries – and this technique rapidly became ubiquitous.

4 The creative members of staff you employ – perhaps not for much longer – will tell you that such electronic enhancement kills innovation. We do not claim that it favours it, but we remind you that, commercially, novelty in itself counts for much less than the illusion of novelty, something you know better than we do. Furthermore, this illusion of novelty is achieved far more easily when existing elements are juxtaposed than by the introduction of radical innovation, in essence destabilising. Revolutionary creativity has never led to sales.

5 Furthermore, the 'artists' lobby will tell you that the consumer will never buy a product known to be automatically generated, and they will be partially right in saying this.

At the risk of being immediately penalised by the market, the systematic use of **ScriptGenerator©®™** to produce content requires the ultimate discretion. However, there is nothing extraordinary about this, manufacturing secrets are the rule in most industries, particularly in the food-processing industry, which once again shows why the practices in force in the entertainment industry need to be brought into line with those of the world economy.

It is, moreover, completely wrong to state that using already existing materials when producing content for the entertainment industry would lead to a fall in consumption. Currently, the most successful products are ones which include details and explanations of their constituent parts – a DVD, for example, will contain a documentary which shows how the feature film was made and extracts of the sources which inspired the filmmaker. These complementary pieces of information are sought out by the public, and it is therefore counter-productive to attempt to hide the fact that the product contains other cultural inputs. On the contrary, details of what has been recycled should be revealed. However, details of how this has been achieved must remain secret.

Natural Gas

It is very hard to determine the details of the image. In the darkness, dozens of shining parallel pipes are lined up, some bathed in electric light, others black, and all around bright trajectories, flashing lights. Outside, an identical structure, rectangles alternately lit or blacked out and luminous arcs, one on top of the other. Any noise which could facilitate an interpretation is muffled by the thick window which gives onto the town. The reflections in the glass, which superimpose the two images, add to the confusion. The computers humming in the trading room are the only sound. The International Petroleum Exchange (IPE) has been closed for the last two hours, the vast room is completely deserted. I have been waiting for half an hour.

Since I came back to London, I have been working once again amidst bright corridors and plain materials. Clattering, rubbing noises, deadened sounds. An invisible film covers the traded material. The city's angles seem to have closed in on themselves momentarily to form a smooth surface upon which I glide as if on a billiard table. And nothing halts the succession of symbols.

My eyes get used to the darkness. I can make out a few angles; translucent bulges of a plastic bottle appear in the middle of a vast whitish projection. Outside, luminous squares gather in rectangular swarms; trajectories are shot through with humming glimmers. I am still waiting.

I am informed at the Chamber of Commerce that Executive Associates, where my predecessor works, is not only a shipping company but also a commercial enterprise. However, Executive Associates is not active in any of the city's stock exchanges – IPE, the London Metal Exchange (LME) or LIFFE (cocoa, coffee, white sugar, potatoes and barley). I contact a number of London traders to find out more, and I am waiting for one of them tonight. He has agreed to meet me at his office. Without going into too much detail and to be sure I would be allowed in, I introduce myself as a financial investigator.

The person I am speaking to has little information to give me about the company I am interested in. Executive Associates never deals directly on the markets but occasionally uses him to effect targeted transactions. The holding company is registered in the Dutch Antilles, and the various subsidiaries in Liberia, Zug and Jersey. He does not know anyone on the Board, not even the Directors based in London. They issue instructions by fax, and the letterhead only gives a PO Box number. Which markets do they tend to deal in? All of them, but not often. They give the impression of being enlightened amateurs; maybe retired traders.

My other contacts are none the wiser. Stranger still, none of the bankers I meet have ever heard of Executive Associates. And yet, raw materials are always traded on a large scale, which requires huge liquid assets. The traders systematically rely on loans. I refuse to believe Executive Associates operates with its own funds. At Bangui, my predecessor must have earned the same salary as me, clearly not enough to engage in international commerce. There can be only two explanations: either his company has its own operations which generate enough profits to cover the deals, or it has other financial assets. But what are they?

I am stymied, nothing progresses. My finances dwindle. The diamonds I brought back from Central Africa are far harder to dispose of in London than in Monrovia. I lose an inordinate amount of time negotiating with middle men who will sell them on in Antwerp. I wait in car parks, subterranean replicas of the offices located above. Everything is the same: plain surfaces; numbered lots, some even assigned; omnipresent surveillance. Transactions initiated upstairs are often concluded downstairs: the exchange of briefcases, business cards and hugs. I join up the dots between yellow switches, green signposts, white lines, grey lamp posts, and draw imaginary figures adrift in the deserted space. A screeching sound, a banging door, the sound of echoing steps soon dissolve these ephemeral constructions.

The intermediary from the Congo wants an exorbitant commission, but he is the only one who agrees to take my uncut diamonds to Antwerp where he will find a cutter and deal on my behalf. Left with nothing, I am forced to accept. He immediately identifies where the stones came from and asks me if the croupier at Bangui Casino was still so beautiful. I say yes – I have never set foot in the Casino – we talk about this and that, the sound of the water dripping from the ceiling prevents us from dragging out any silences, we have to open up a bit. He explains that he has been using small dinghies to traffic petrol between Central Africa and the Brazzaville-Congo for ages, he apologises for his rates, he needs money to go home. Family? Business, he has a problem to sort out. Diamonds? Petrol. Well, not exactly, gas in fact. He hesitates: is methane a gas or petrol? More a gas. What is it about? I can perhaps be of help (anything to get a better price for my diamonds).

Two days later, I am waiting for him on a bench at Canary Wharf. New office buildings under construction regularly carve up the narrow network of London's old docks. In front of me, pillars of a new building shrouded by a network of metal scaffolding are covered in fine meshed wire to protect them from the dust. The gently blowing wind brings this foamy snowdrift to life. On the shiny pavement which turns a reddish colour beneath the street lights, the dirty snow looks like a ball of grease on the back of a carved-up fish. The intermediary will also speak about snow. Frozen white balls recovered from the depths of the Atlantic burn the moment they are ignited. Methane hydrate, in fact. Volumes of this substance, but more specifically shiploads of methane initially located 5,000 metres below the surface, have been extracted 800 kilometres off the Congo coast. Two methane tankers are waiting in Matadi harbour for the Congo government to authorise delivery of this precious cargo to Asia. But the paperwork does not arrive. Geologists who have been involved in the work estimate that the extracted materials provide valuable information about how the African continent was formed, and more specifically on the genesis of the Congo River. The methane was found amidst concentric circles of debris which open out from the river mouth in the alluvial cone of the water flow, and which have formed a logbook of fluvial activity over the course of several million years. The scientists want to recover the cargo for analysis, and the traders, who have already sold the gas, want to close the deal. They have asked my interlocutor to get things moving in Kinshasa.

The story is far too complicated – I don't think I can be of any use given that, to my knowledge, I have never studied the composition of methane hydrate. I have to resign myself to take a big hit selling my diamonds. The go-between will go to Antwerp tomorrow and he will leave for the Congo at the end of the week. And like all true mules, he will swallow the stones. In Bangui, some cut themselves and insert the diamonds into their wounds before covering it all up with a plaster. Only I believe my gems are safe, squeezed in between the silver paper and the cardboard of my packet of cigarettes.

We walk. The forgotten names of East India Docks and Spice Walk answer to the sound of our whispering. We stumble upon heaps of piled-up shadows; we can hear the rusty cranes jingling. In a service station cafeteria, we quickly draw up authentication certificates for my stones. To explain their provenance, without arousing too much suspicion, we invent a straightforward journey without too many legs and include the names of recognised dealers with the odd spelling mistake. The inspectors will fall for the errors and in the event of an investigation, we can always plead the document was drawn up in good faith. On the table, embers in a disposable cup. Through the misted windows, circling the petrol pumps, black and silky masses sway with the slowness of huge sea beds. The shade is speckled with stars of wet plankton.

Uneasy return journey. Just before I leave my go-between, I discover that the company responsible for sending him to the Congo is none other than Executive Petroleum, the Swiss subsidiary of Executive Associates.

He also lets slip that the money used to buy the methane has been obtained in exchange for a mortgage. This resolves the liquidity issue: Executive Associates did not raise a loan but mortgaged goods or shares. Maybe the manual printed on the watery green-coloured laminated paper, of which only the first two pages are in my possession. No doubt the missing sections describe a system to quickly generate colossal profits.

6 The constraints **ScriptGenerator©®™** imposes on these raw materials are those of the marketplace. Hence, in order to add maximum value, the software always uses the same formula, which follows some basic principles. This formula is a guarantee; all content produced by **ScriptGenerator©®™** will exhibit four essential characteristics:

1 simplicity, in order that the most varied alloys can be enriched and refined

2 flexibility, to allow for episodes, follow-ups and sequels

3 universal appeal, to enable overseas sales

4 apparent originality, which allows the consumer to be surprised but never disconcerted.

7 The only formula which perfectly satisfies these four requirements is the quest. The structure is simple – an individual or a group of individuals search for an object, a character, or a solution, which is found following a series of ups and downs. A quest relies on only three different materials: the investigator, the sought-after object and the narrative units which link the one to the other. The cost of materials required for a quest, therefore, is low. Starting from three components, an infinite number of variations present themselves. A detective story is obtained by making the sought-after object a murderer. For a romantic story, it is a case of bringing two lovers together. The horror, fantasy and other such genres are produced by means of a straightforward reversal: here,

it is the sought-after object that pursues the investigator.

8 The way the elements of a quest are organised also allows the product to be adapted to all media; this is done by simply modulating the parameters in response solely to economic demands. **ScriptGenerator©®™** provides additional episodes if you need to meet the demands of television, which finances series by the season. To satisfy the graphic demands of a video game, **ScriptGenerator©®™** can add characters and sought-after objects. If you want to make a film, **ScriptGenerator©®™** reduces the number of plotlines. And so on.

9 It is a waste of time to discuss the universal appeal of the quest model; it's obvious. However, given this truth, other genres are affected by their cultural specificity.

10 The quest model allows apparent originality, a crucial factor for the entertainment industry. This complex requirement can be summarised as follows: in order to be successful, a cultural product has to present to the consumer a known quantity in an unexpected manner. The quest lends itself particularly well to this delicate exercise, as originality in this case does not depend on its structure, which is too obvious to confuse the consumer. The more complicated plots, formatted as quests, work on the condition that at least one (but never more than two) of the constituent elements must not, under any circumstances, be original but must belong to known universes. Let us consider a few examples:

1 A woman (sought-after element, commonplace) disappears and her husband (investigator, commonplace) goes in search of her. New twist in the tale: she has not really disappeared, she has merely become invisible.

2 A group of terrorists (investigator, commonplace) sets out to destroy a series of famous monuments in a given country (sought-after element, commonplace) whilst this very same group of terrorists had previously been trained and funded by the Secret Services of this very same country (plotline, original).

3 In a completely foreign universe, unidentifiable in time or space (plotline, original), a caste of warriors resembling, by all accounts, an oriental order (investigator, commonplace) is looking for the weak spot of an empire which has all the characteristics of a Nazi regime (sought-after element, commonplace) in order to eliminate it.

11 This way of operating dictates that all classification by type (novel, story, play, poem, etc.), which is of no use to the production of content, be abandoned. The same applies to the distinction between real and imaginary. (However, the software will inform you if the use of real events presents copyright problems; if not, it will not distinguish between real and fictitious components.) These obsolete categories are replaced by genres, with the approval of the marketplace:

romance, adventure, suspense, horror, 'arthouse', detective, drama, etc. Bookshops and video rental shops already use these categories. In fact, the consumer already shows a preference for categorising by genre because it provides prior-to-purchase information on the contents. Who knows what to expect when buying a 'novel', a collection of 'poems'? Buying a 'thriller' is unambiguous though there remains a surprise element to the product. The consumer, in fact, knows that some unexpected elements will feature in the intrigue, the characters or the mood. Apparent originality, we repeat, is the real key to the entertainment industry, which is why **ScriptGenerator©®™** is the best adapted production tool for this sector of the economy.

Cotton

There was nothing memorable about him. Both his appearance and his face were completely anodyne. I may well have been irritated by his extreme slowness had I been behind him on a staircase or in a corridor. I would have forgotten him instantly, though, for he lacked any obvious characteristics which might add to my impatience. I was drunk, I was wandering around one of the corridors in the Underground and I fainted. When I came to, he was crouching down, touching my skull, his eyes half closed. I pushed him away violently; he set off without even looking at me, rubbing his fingers against each other.

Here he is again. He is sitting on a bench; he seems to be watching the passers-by. But he uses his right hand to smooth out an abandoned piece of newspaper stained with grease. The crossword grid and the numbered clues are still decipherable in the greyish sodden pulp. Some breadcrumbs and bits of chips are folded in the paper. He repeatedly runs his fingers over the paper, rubbing them against each other. He gets up, I follow him. May as well try to trail smoke; I lose him.

I am virtually incapable of describing him. I think he was quite old, but I am not even sure whether he was wearing glasses. I run my fingers through my hair, what was he looking for? I find a discreet scar line, a few bumps, a bit of sand and some fibres. I am completely preoccupied with the results of the sale of my diamonds. I hang out in bars where traders, with no enthusiasm, come to get drunk once the markets have closed. However, still no news. I stay in a corner reading and rereading that soya and corn values are going south on the Chicago Board of Trade. Most of my neighbours, small investors, do the same, oblivious to their surroundings. The strangest among this colony, made up of people who, now that they are retired, have much more time on their hands, is a blind man who is listening on a small portable radio to the market reports. He is speculating on cotton, both on the New York and Osaka Exchanges. Given the fifteen-hour time difference between the two places, he sleeps little.

Suddenly he grasps hold of my arm: there is a dead spot in this room, tell me where it is, it must be in this direction. He points to the benches at the back. A trader, his mouth open, is asleep there. The man from the night before, seated next to him, repeatedly runs his fingers over his teeth, his gums and his lips. His eyes are closed as they were when he was feeling my skull. No one has noticed what he is up to. I describe the scene to the blind man; tell him about the character's earlier appearance. He is intrigued, informs me that he can sense him quite clearly, like a shrivelled eye swimming above a sea of sounds. He has just stood up. Correct: would he tail him with me? Why not, Osaka has just closed. I leave the City, the blind man leaning on my arm. My guide is confident and he takes no notice of the white lines, the arrows and the flashing lights. I am lost almost immediately. The man stops a few times to rub his cheek against a poster. Further on, he removes his shoes to trample on a pile of dry leaves piled up in a corner. He is not wearing any socks, but continues to stamp for a while. He sets off again, picks up a sodden piece of rope covered in tar, which he stuffs into his pocket. He leans up against a wall and stays there without moving whilst he methodically runs his two hands over a few centimetres of powdery stone. Stops suddenly, to collect with a knife some dust which has accumulated on the contours of a carving on the front of a door.

We leave London along long suburban streets. Standing upright in front of a door, his hand on the doorknob, the man we have been following beckons us to come in. All the windows in the house are covered with heavy curtains. We cross the threshold, mind the step.

There is no furniture; all the rooms are lined from floor to ceiling with white ceramic tiles. He throws three cushions on the floor, and invites us to sit down. It is the first time he has been followed right to his front door; the situation has never arisen before. The bell rings and, smiling at our sudden anxiety, he goes to open the door and comes back with a tray filled with cups of tea and biscuits. He asks us a few questions, and then answers the questions himself; he speaks quickly, and his voice, at times, is inaudible. Whilst he talks he crumbles biscuits onto the floor. You are not the first to question my behaviour, no, not the first. Usually I give the curious the slip, I have ways of escape. Your tenacity is hard to explain, I know how good I am. Your sound imprint is distinctive, interjects the blind man. Of course I know all this but this imprint, as you call it, is hollow. A lack, the ear misses a step. It appears you have tracked this silence. Very annoying. Disturbing, truly disturbing.

He is currently rolling the piece of rope picked up on the way into the biscuit crumbs. The biscuit debris adheres to the tar.

About his work: I am looking for fluffy tar. Ideally, bitumen flakes. First, I experiment, I fiddle around, and then I reinvent it in the laboratory. Do you create materials? (It is the first time I have spoken.) No, not create, I simply combine them. I remember sensations well, so I remix them to see what happens. Laminated chalk, dust from wool. Without any goal? Initially with nothing in mind, I was bored by being enclosed, I had to do something. Then there were partners, artisans at first, new fabrics. Then came the industrialists. I am housed, fed, dressed, no questions asked, and in exchange I produce. Softer plastics, creams, stronger shampoos, glasses, new woods. I do not alter the properties; I am incapable of making a harder metal, I change what things feel like. My laboratory is in the cellar.

Do you produce for everyone? Only for one company, who then sells on. And then suddenly: I am very expensive, you know, I am insured for several million dollars.

An idea: what are your partners' names? Silence; he only knows the two scientists who come to collect his products every week. As it happens they are expected any time now. Could we meet them? That is why I invited you in, I would like to work with you (he speaks to the blind man), but I need their consent. The blind man does not say no, and the other one says he is not terribly gifted with sounds and that he is increasingly asked for powders which hiss, cotton that does not rustle, and cardboard which crackles. My presence seems to have been forgotten, and I avoid drawing attention to it.

To pass the time, we visit the laboratory – flasks, sinks, test tubes and at the far end of the room, thousands of labelled shoe boxes piled up against the wall, 'ashes of silk', 'dried stone jelly', etc. The ceramic tiles on the work surfaces seem to have taken over the house like a virus. The sleeping partners arrive later on, their white overalls clearly visible beneath their raincoats, glasses, hair closely cropped, leather suitcases which, when placed on the ground, let out a sound of clinking glass (no doubt test tubes inside). They appear indifferent to me and to the blind man's presence, they catch up on news from our lacklustre host (Are you sleeping OK? Do you like the food?). After a few minutes, our host introduces the blind man to them and tells them about his plan. This man has exceptional hearing; I would like him to take up residence here and for him to be treated in the same way as I am. He could help me with some of the work on the materials and sounds you have given me: you know as well as I do that I will not be able to manage on my own.

Silence. One of the two sleeping partners asks to take delivery for the previous orders as authorized, and goes down to the laboratory. The other one asks the blind man if he wants to negotiate alone. He points at me: this gentleman will discuss the details with you, I will stay here. So, I then leave the cold store disguised as a suburban house with the two men in white overalls and get into the back of their car. Outside it is still dark, and not a single word will be uttered during the journey. Views of the roads, avenues, pylons, shadowy lines of the pavements wind around the car like a fairground, threads of candyfloss around sticks. Even later on, from the windows of the small jet which takes us to Switzerland (the canton of Zug), the threads which make up the highway appear to scroll around themselves before finally forming relatively loose urban balls of wool.

Disembarked from the plane, I spend seemingly endless hours in the waiting room of an office located close to the airport. Long enough for me to realise that I am at the head office of Executive Sciences, a Swiss subsidiary of Executive Associates. After a while, two men.

Of course, we cannot offer your protégé a similar contract to the one we have with our man. In fact, the agreement we have with him is more supervisory than anything else. We can offer you a standard consultant's contract, automatically renewable, with performance-linked payments. The blind man will have access to various services (accommodation, full board) and these will be deducted from his wage. However, we would rather all transactions take place outside the United Kingdom. Do you have a Swiss bank account? No, however I do still have an account in Mauritius which dates back to my old mining days. That's perfect. We will place the orders ourselves and will take receipt of the results. We will only contact you in the event of a problem. Sign here.

Handshake, index finger pressure on the lift's *Rez-de-Chaussée* button, outside, a snowy day, raw and as uniform as neon. At least I have one foot in the door. As the blind man's improvised agent, I have a salary – the sale of my diamonds now seems less important – and I now have a valid reason to interest myself in what goes on at Executive Associates.

Hotel room. Bright lines, raw materials, dull colour. The only real piece of furniture in the room is the huge bay window which takes up the whole of a wall and gives out onto the ski slopes. In a few minutes a storm comes up, blurring the contours of the landscape. Very quickly, no more sky, mountains or snow, but only a vast fresco of water vapour at various degrees of freezing. This mixed shading of grey is dappled by fleeting darker shadows, but perhaps they are merely whirlwinds.

To sum up: to all intents and purposes, it is not the manual printed on a watery green-coloured glazed paper on which Executive Associates were taking a punt on, but on the man, located in the suburb, who makes up materials which will garnish tomorrow's supermarket shelves. The initial question – where is the manual, and what use do they make of it? – remains unanswered. Seated on my bed in light refracted by the window – it looks half the size since the storm started – I reread the first two pages.

12 To maximise use, thousands of components accrued in the **ScriptGenerator©®™** database are ranked according to plot utility. **ScriptGenerator©®™** entries are initially sorted into three main categories: investigator, the sought-for object and the innovative ups and downs; these also make up the three basic categories for the quest model. The composition of each category never changes. An investigator is not defined by what he does or what he feels but by his physical and intellectual characteristics. These traits add up to form a type – thoughtless seducer, fighter, ordinary person easily overwhelmed by events, etc – that remains unchanged throughout the quest. The definition of the sought-after object, like that of the invesigator, is made through its characteristics, such as its properties, source of healing, wealth, etc. The events are organised around three axes: their significance in the final product, their long-term implications for how the quest evolves, and the number of components they incorporate. For example, the introduction of a chase or a shooting will have little effect on the rest of the product, but will have a significant role to play during the quest itself and will require the use of numerous components. The discovery of a clue, however, will be a virtually instantaneous element, relying on only one or two components, and will immediately affect the plotline and will have severe consequences for whatever follows.

Once the overall format of the product has been validated, **ScriptGenerator©®™** generates a one-page synopsis for presentation to your Board of Directors. This synopsis will serve to inform products of the marketing campaign: posters, p.o.s., shelf-wobblers, etc

13 The next phase is the development of a range of spin-offs to enrich the core product. Listed amongst the components on offer, you will find 'characteristics' (which include physical appearance, biography, and a glossary of the terms used), 'atmospherics' (décors, surroundings and moods), 'human environment' (which refers to the characters who range from extras to those in secondary roles, all of whom are defined in as much detail as the central characters, so as to be ready for development in a future volume), 'trials' (stunts, fights, various traps), 'gadgets' (key elements of the décor and punch lines, a particularly useful category for the insertion of a sponsor's message), etc.

14 You will note that **ScriptGenerator©®™** uses a classification system which is the same as that used by traders in raw materials; the components are ranked by use and not by their intrinsic properties. The hierarchy is dynamic: initially every component can be a key element of the quest, but once these have been identified, any element not selected automatically becomes secondary. This first transaction between you and **ScriptGenerator©®™** determines how the software will rank its components, and not some intrinsic value of the materials (see also paragraph 1).

15 In marked contrast to the few attempts already made at a systemised production tool, **ScriptGenerator©®™** exercises great care to process all the elements which make up the content, and does not focus exclusively on the overall composition of the product. Claims to expand so-called 'pulp' content in fact consist of finding a 'hit' formula, an unchanging model of intrigue, built around a few recurring characters, with the use of a technician to fill in the cracks between the selected elements. This method, even if it does contain some similarities with ours, generally leads to disastrous results. The technician's intervention inevitably means the inclusion of arbitrary or improbable elements, the inclusion of which can only be justified by the former's 'inspiration'. A good formula can also be ruined by a mishmash of ideas, which do not sell, as was the case for many early twentieth-century serialised novels. Products as promising as *Fantômas* or *Arsene Lupin*, ironically found themselves celebrated by numerous artists because of the freedom enjoyed by their 'creators'! However, to be adapted for television or cinema, these contents had to be completely reformatted.

Contrary to these craft methods, our software allows you to define your entire content, right down to the smallest detail. We have been influenced by our experience in the coffee markets. A grain trader, when dealing with the food industry, does not just offer his clients one type of coffee, he does everything in his power to sell a whole range of different beans (Robusta, Arabica, etc) from all the different producer countries (Brazil, Vietnam, Cameroon, Colombia, etc) to be used in the making up of their product. The majority of coffees commercially available are mixes ('Blends') made up of many different types of beans. In the same way, **ScriptGenerator©®™** perfectly balances the public's expectations with the range of available materials.

Sugar

The burnished spout of a teapot emerging from a clod of earth is protected by a Plexiglas cube. Beneath it a small label, 'Algiers, 2001'. Further away, a cold room conceals a few items normally found in a wardrobe – socks, underwear and shirt – frozen in a block of ice. The caption reads 'Chamonix, December 1981'. There is also a rearview mirror protruding from the trunk of a palm tree – 'Barbados, 1987'; a section on the wall reveals clearly an outline created by a very powerful flash – 'Baghdad, 1991'; a fishing-net solidified by some dried petrol – 'Belle-Ile, 1998'; and a computer keyboard covered with shells and algae – 'Banjul, 1987' .

The exhibition takes up the entire hall of the hotel; it is not publicised anywhere: neither poster nor prospectus, neither signature nor explanatory information. In any event I am the only one to take a close look at these relics.

To the right, the dining room. Because of the storm, nothing outside is visible. The windows are uniformly covered with a snowy mother of pearl effect; we are in a conch, footsteps echo. No one here either. I help myself to the breakfast buffet, untouched despite the late hour. In the middle of the vast room, a domestic appliance, hard to identify because black and partly melted, stands on a pedestal. However, amongst the streaks of soot and the molten metal some switches and an internal cavity encrusted with carbon can be made out – 'Gaza, 1999'. Probably an oven or a freezer.

Further, the sitting room. A woman dozes in an armchair. I sit down next to the window. A man enters. He is talking in hushed tones into a mobile phone and he is carrying an expenses book under his arm. He walks around the metal casting which stands on a half column just at the entrance to the room; it has a cast iron surround, and engraved onto the glass surface, in the Cyrillic alphabet – 'Barents Sea, 1999'. Once his conversation is over, he sits down on a sofa, places his exercise book on his knees and diligently writes on the left-hand page. He then dials a number on his telephone, gets up, and, pacing up and down, talks to the person at the other end of the line, hangs up and goes back to his exercise book, only this time, he writes on the right-hand page. He tears out the two pages, folds them in four and comes up to me. Excuse me; do you think you could...? He points to the fireplace and hands me the two pieces off paper. My wife normally takes care of these things, but she is asleep... I cross the room and throw the paper into the fire. He repeats the exercise four times: phone, left-hand page, phone, right-hand page, apologetic smile, fireplace. The wind lashes the windows with snow, studding the glass with stars.

He comes up to me again. I try to take control of the situation: Could you possibly explain to me what the point of...? He smiles, asks me if I know where the exhibits on display in the hotel come from.

The owner is an ex-member of the International Red Cross life-saving commandoes, he brought back a sample of each one of his expeditions from around the world. With bad grace, I move towards the fireplace, slip the two pieces of paper into my pocket, and, instead of the document I was given, I throw a prospectus onto the flames and leave the sitting room, waving over my shoulder.

On my floor at the end of the corridor, in a small cabinet recessed in the wall, basic toiletries – razor, nail scissors, metal hairbrush – emerge from a piece of lava: 'Reykjavik, 1993'.

It quickly becomes apparent that this hotel is not in the business of putting people up. I have to demand my first bill, and I never ask for a second one. Empty corridors. The doors of the immaculate rooms are always left open. Occasionally two men in the sauna. A group talking in hushed tones at the far end of the dining room. Four people make their way on the golf course without really playing. Silent couples in the sitting room. Every one treats me with the utmost kindness, as if I were a member of the inner circle who had got up to go to the bathroom and for whom the others wait before ordering their coffee. It's a good situation to be in, but it makes asking to be enlightened difficult. People start conversations with me easily, but as soon as it becomes obvious that I don't know anything, they change the subject.

Therefore I can only guess that the man I saw yesterday on television giving a press conference to the Zug Council is not only a local politician, but also is on the board of a trading company, given that he is smoking a cigar with some businessmen at the hotel. That the woman who at breakfast time comes to read her notes to a group of silent men is close to an important person. That the elegant octogenarian who is presented with a dish of black substances in the dining room must be a food taster at the famous palace, and is responsible for identifying the genuine provenance of the discounted shipments. And that the man with the mobile phone whom I met on the first day performs the difficult role of alibi for the brokers. For a price, he lets them use his name on the paper, fictitiously buys and sells merchandise, destroys any trace of it and consequently is identified with either the first or the last stage in a series of deals. This system allows the buyers and sellers to declare, without lying, that they are ignorant of the origins or the final destination of their produce. The exchange, which I managed to miss the last bit of, refers to a shipment of coltan, a mineral used in mobile phone microchips and currently subject of an international embargo as it is extracted from a war zone, the frontier between the Congo and Rwanda. This hotel is a smoke screen, a gigantic machine to fictionalise matter.

No one seems bothered by the snowdrifts which accumulate in the parking lot, the dusty gusts which cloud windows and block doors, or the ice which threatens to burst the pipes. The hotel is being immersed in snow whilst at its very centre, a hoard of people buzz around busily chewing over and regurgitating matter. Tons of sisal and wool go from one room to the next, leaving a few balls of fibre beneath the beds. The lifts shoot up and down relentlessly and despatch cargoes of petrol from Angola to Spain. Quintals of barley and wheat run through the plumbing and air conditioning circuit, occasionally showering a surprised guest with cereal. When the musak stops on the ground floor, one can hear the muffled cries of the sheep and the pigs, their legs attached to a rolling winch on rails fixed to the corridor, making their way across continents to reach the abattoirs. If you get up before the chambermaids come round, you will see light streaks of blood on the plinths.

And always, in these shops and warehouses, the same characters dressed in black and grey, in neutral suits. Always the same colonies, industrious and stubborn. They sniff the hectolitres of milk in the swimming pool, the cocoa beans hidden beneath damp washing, in the laundry. They grab them and transform them amidst a rustling of mandibles. They then leave, walking backwards, carefully erasing any evidence of their passage. A swarm similar to the one I see every day produced the printed manual on watery green-coloured glazed paper. I have managed to infiltrate their hideout but, paradoxically, it is now harder to know where the pages are subsequent to the first two I now know by heart. I go round and round in circles in this muted hotel. I will use a meeting in Rotterdam to pick up the proceeds of my diamond sale as the reason for my departure, a convenient and equally artificial pretext.

16 Production software, **ScriptGenerator©®™**, of course, conforms to all economic restrictions imposed by the entertainment business. Each option on offer is carefully calculated. The cost of any given selection, its potential financial viability, copyright fees as well as potential royalties, is carefully evaluated. This function, which assesses the benefits and the investment required, is determined by the end product: **ScriptGenerator©®™** assesses differently a comic strip, a video game or a book.

17 **ScriptGenerator**©®™ has another function which will be particularly useful for your financial projections: it can calculate a product's potential. **ScriptGenerator©®™** will estimate your project's potential success by comparing the structure and its components with other similar and previously released products.

ScriptGenerator©®™ will inform you if it lacks enough data to estimate the profitability of an element, and will suggest a range of solutions which will resolve the uncertainty of the issue (market research, product testing, etc). If, for example, you wanted to launch a book which focuses on a young, uninhibited woman's quest for sexual pleasure, **ScriptGenerator©®™** would inform you that your product has every likelihood of selling well, given the success of similar works already written on this theme – particularly in France. It would also suggest ways of integrating the main components found in products already on the market into your product, whilst at the same time, slightly differentiating your product.

18 This function, which calculates potential sales figures, does not simply operate by analysing competing products. ZEITGEIST, an index unique to **ScriptGenerator©®™**, features prominently in the profit and loss assessment. This index constantly measures the frequency with which themes, imagery and characters appear in the media or in a cultural context, and it allows you to integrate them in your productions. The ZEITGEIST index ensures that you do not miss any current trends and allows you to position yourself in a market before it becomes saturated. The ZEITGEIST index precisely measures the frequency of the elements it features: if the frequency is too high, you will be dissuaded from using it, since it is likely to bomb.

19 The ZEITGEIST index has been conceived to eradicate one of the last remaining arguments used by creatives, whose salaries – which take a large chunk out of your budget – are justified by their supposed ability to identify emerging fashions and imagery. Some of you have already outflanked this final attempt by the 'artists' to justify their existence by simply buying up niche production units (cultzine, art gallery, independent publisher) and by incorporating them into your conglomerate and using them as a source of r & d. **ScriptGenerator©®™** pushes this strategy one step further – with favourable results – by replacing the creatives' so-called 'flair' with a carefully honed statistical tool.

20 Lastly, the results produced by the ZEITGEIST index are useful in one aspect of the production process which cannot – and should not – be automated: marketing. The trends and gaps in the market highlighted by the index will help you to further refine your sales strategy, and launch new advertising campaigns which will perfectly match the market's expectations. As a result, a large number of conglomerates who started by using **ScriptGenerator©®™** in their financial departments, asked us to adapt the software so that it could be used by their marketing departments. With this synergy, it has been possible for selling points to be incorporated very early on in the production process and in samplers of the product launched to test the water, before rolling out the final product. Some groups have even opted to include in new products information concerning forthcoming products – e.g., books will end with the first chapter of the next book in the series.

Maritime Freight Index

On the docks, the piled-up containers perfectly blend in with the landscape of the buildings of the nearby Rotterdam suburb. The same colours – blue and burgundy – for the crates and the housing estates, the same numbers – registration or stairwell, same cranes, same dashes of neon accentuating the outlines, same shadows which stray and scribble on the walls. The containers reproduce the layout of the far-off suburbs where they have been loaded; the docks offer us a brief image of Abidjan or Kuala Lumpur. Undeveloped harbour wasteland, which could have crossed the oceans fugitively, becomes for a few hours the exact reflection of other wasteland. In the city, an entire city is dismantled in the morning, when the unidentified blocks of merchandise are loaded onto pallets belonging to the trucks waiting a few metres away.

The operations room for Executive Freight, a 'transport' subsidiary of Executive Associates, looks like a video surveillance centre. Inside the operations room, the location signs, radio announcements and video flux invade the intimacy of the truck cabins. Windowless, the room can focus on whichever European motorway the drivers call out. On this skiff tossed about by radio waves, some ten traders negotiate cargo in real time. One essential fact: real profits are made on the sale of merchandise already in circulation. Delivery alone yields nothing. Cargo already in transit, on motorways, over the seas, on trains, is sold many times over, and it is only once the trailer is unhitched in the early hours of the morning that the transaction ends. The trucks then have to be re-loaded as quickly as possible, for fear of the profit margins being immediately eroded.

The truckers never come in here (though they park next door), but this only becomes apparent from the corridor which, open on one side, gives onto the neighbouring car park. Then the image of the estates returns: the private surveillance, the flashing lights, the frenetically scattered groups and banks of light, constant and orange, which highlight every detail, like those children, fugitive as some retinal image, who try to disappear in a skip. A genuine fear of stowaways fills the air. And their desire, often realised through great physical contortions, is to lose themselves in the merchandise. Executive Freight is in fact officially run by one of them, whose status is now legal.

In a soft voice, with an unidentifiable accent, he explains that clandestinity is the only way to really get to know the road. The alternative is to read a map. And what's more, you know how the merchandise inside the containers will behave. The flour which goes mouldy at the bottom of the vats, the bumps which thaw the frozen goods, motor fuel which seeps out on the road, bananas which ripen if the temperature rises by one or two degrees (the slightest body contact turns them yellow beneath your very eyes, and you learn how to spread your body out over the shipment to have enough to eat during the crossing).

How many journeys before getting here? Ten or so, but always completed before the deadline. The tenth time I was discovered here turned into a job interview. They were impressed by my knowledge of the Central Asia routes, essential for reaching Dubai and Turkey. The docks of the Iranian port of Bandar-e'Abbas, opposite Dubai, the watch-towers between Armenia and Turkey (every five hundred meters) and the transit zones in Georgia. But others – he points his chin towards two of his colleagues – have experienced river flows between countries, four of them on an inflatable tyre, their possessions in a plastic bag and their legs inflamed by industrial mud and chemical waste. Or even squashed up next to a dead animal, a red veil in front of one's eyes, whether the lids are open or closed. And there you have it. The gesture indicates the white rectangular spaces on the parking-lot, a way of containing the endlessly moving land.

On the wall behind him, dozens of drawings, similar to the maps highlighting emergency exits, hang. They describe the various ways in which the stowaways try to climb into vehicles. Highlighted in thick black lines, illegal aliens are shown squatting at the bottom of a tank, clutching the chassis of a trailer, hidden in various machines – freezers and cars, in particular – etc. Each drawing is coded: a poster displays the real events that refer to the code number. The merchandise is specified, the place of discovery and the likely place the stowaways gained access.

I spend a long time on this hyper-coded terrain where everything is a sign and where nothing is legible. Brownish flow, stenches, gas, smoke, sudden alarm call. A deafening and repetitive crash, then suddenly nothing, and this language made up of acronyms and registration numbers that were already in use in Buchanan, in Liberia. The assembly and disassembly of the container buildings seem to happen without the slightest human intervention, amidst the regular bangings of the cranes and the pulsations of the pipes. There is always the fear of trespassing, as nothing is signposted, the ground is unmarked, and only defined by a few puddles and grazes. Differentiated only by the size and height of the material they conceal: solids (hangar), liquids (vat) or gases (balloons). The building's functions are unclear; simple containers.

And even then this classification is only approximate. But how to find out? Nothing leaks here, leaks belong on the high seas, black wakes of tanks emptying, or later on, on the roads, the rail tracks. The crates fall, and suddenly the pulses, the beans swell and blacken beneath the rain, like a pile of gravel. Nothing stays in the harbour long enough to seep out, other than the boats themselves which rot offshore.

It is there, in the rusty holds of the *Pola*, a wreck registered in Panama, that I will meet up with the intermediary who sold my stones in Antwerp. To go down into the hold, I use a rotten ladder which crumbles beneath my feet. Electrical equipment purrs in a corner of this empty inverted metallic nave. There is a table, covered with portable computers and mobile phones. In addition to my intermediary, a man and a woman are seated. I want to greet them, but my intermediary stops me by raising a finger to his mouth. He takes an envelope out of his jacket and hands it to me. I stuff it in my pocket without counting the notes and, aware of the fact that I am not welcome, I prepare to leave. But a chair is indicated and coffee served. The tank echoes; it's impossible to say whether this is caused by the ebb and flow of the foam or by the pigeons flapping their wings. In contrast to the black shadows on the internal partitions of the hull, the light spreads itself out, evenly, from no discernible source. Mineralised, it forms a mound in the centre of the hold. On its flanks, cigarette smoke gathers and flows down.

I recognise the woman, I saw her in Zug. She was with the unmemorable negotiator who installed himself in the hotel lounge where I was staying; it was she whose place I took when I threw the pieces of paper in the fireplace. She does not have the time to remember me; a man comes down the ladder. He takes a batch of papers from his bag, divides it up into four piles of equal size, slides them into folders made of bakelite, which he seals with a metal band, hands them to us. My batch consists of some fifty pages of glazed watery green paper. It's at this point that the woman recognises me and smiles.

21 All contents and components archived in the **ScriptGenerator©®™** memory are protected by user rights. Thanks to a function developed by the best lawyers, our software will alert you to the status of each element. If, for example, you select a scene for your product which includes Royal Canadian Mounted Police officers or Ghurkhas (elite corps in the British army), **ScriptGenerator©®™** will highlight the cost of using this image. But the software will equally advise you of all the available ways to reduce, even eliminate, these costs. So, if you decide to re-use the script of an already existing content – *Gone with the Wind*, for example – **ScriptGenerator©®™** will not only inform you how much the rights will cost, but it will also compare this amount with the costs incurred should a complaint be lodged by those who hold the rights to the product (together with the probability of such a complaint being lodged).

ScriptGenerator©®™ will always select the cheapest option.

22 A not negligible part of the contents and components of **ScriptGenerator©®™** is not protected, either because it has only just come onto the market, or because its status is not clearly defined. For your Board of Directors to be confident that the products you will be presenting them with are not legally problematic, **ScriptGenerator©®™** provides a function which allows you to acquire them. This is in effect a virtual commodity exchange, which brings together, online, all the software users, and organises auctions of the contents and components for those of our clients who are interested. This exchange uses its own staff to put buyers and sellers in contact with each other and organise the market. It is a supply and demand system, which is transparent, open only to you and to your main competitors, and it helps prevent numerous legal conflicts, which are specifically related to the acquisition of uncertain rights, and also limits price rises. It is not in the market's interest that bids go too high or that a particular vendor acquire too much power.

23 Not only is this first-ever unified system for buying and reselling rights very practical, the exchange accessed by **ScriptGenerator©®™** users also has another advantage: it is open to all types of products. You can acquire contents and components which are itemised in the **ScriptGenerator©®™** database whose other media rights (in the case of a book or article, this would be the film rights) have yet to be negotiated, but above all you can have access to new contents. Thus, documents created by individuals following a spectacular event – photos, amateur videos, recordings, oral descriptions – are immediately available on the **ScriptGenerator©®™** exchange. The same applies for personal accounts of life stories, accidents, illnesses, phobias or perversions, which can be very useful for the 'reality' category (whether in an audiovisual, radio or print format). Each time a new product comes up for sale, you are notified in real time, and given the opportunity to state your intention to bid.

24 This exchange for contents and components functions in much the same way as the commodity market: it offers a whole range of financial tools which enable the buyer to anticipate market risk. Either you can make 'spot' purchases (where acquisition and payment are immediate) or draw up term contracts (where the delivery date is set at a period of three or six months, even a year).

25 As the exchange is a central feature of **ScriptGenerator©®™**, it of course adopts all the codes **ScriptGenerator©®™** uses and only sells formatted contents and components. Personal accounts, events, tales and different events are thus systematically broken down into the 'investigator', 'quest' and 'events' categories.

Electricity

Initially, disjointed elements. Reflections of transformers, stable yet precarious apparitions on the lake's surface. The frieze of debris runs along the reservoir. Here and there, cadavers of blackened monkeys, electrified. Mist hangs over the dam like ivy on a wall, ghostly. Air full of grit.

I exactly copy my companions' movements. I did this throughout the journey. It's the only thing they asked of me. They have spent years transporting all sorts of documents and money in their little black leather bags. It would take too long to explain to you, we follow lots of little routines to get through check points successfully, just copy us. So, in queues I respected the distance set between the four of us; I did not look at them once, I asked the taxis to follow their cars, and never provided more information than I was asked for. During this time I conjured up an image in my mind of variegated volumes containing all the printed sheets of paper they had shifted during their career. Millions of coded sheets of paper. Bricks of obscure and secret sediment, revealed by an investigation or a raid, exposed like a ray of light penetrating a cloud of cigarette smoke.

They did not answer any of my questions. They did not want to tell me who they were working for, nor the purpose of the journey. The presence of my intermediary leads me to suspect some connection with Executive Associates; they could be messengers, but this hypothesis is impossible to prove. Only the woman offered me the choice of staying in Rotterdam. This time, I chose not to answer.

We go round the lake, and head for the dam. The command centre overhangs the valley, embedded in the middle of a concrete cliff, on the opposite side of the lake. To reach it one has to use an iron walkway and cross over some turbines, operating so fast it is impossible to assess their speed. Pistons swarm in the semi-darkness, straps move, reptile-like, and the water seethes. At the end of the last corridor, a final presentation of documents, one last search, and an armour-plated door is opened. On the other side of the door, a trading-room. Some fifty traders, mirroring the aquatic twists of the dam's mechanism, bustle about selling electricity produced by the complex to all neighbouring countries. There are quotes – for immediate delivery and futures contracts – computers, and telephones. Covering one of the walls, a vast map of South-East Asia details all the distribution networks and power stations, brighter or paler red dots reflecting the hourly output. Nobody takes any notice of us.

Finally, we are questioned. The person you are looking for is not here, she is in the film studios, opposite the dam. Follow this man: he will take you there. We retrace our steps; our guide wears an orange overall, like all the warehousemen here. On the other side of the lake, the workmen wear the same uniform; the same company manages both the dam and the studios. The turbines also supply the film shoots.

There is no apparent activity. Only huge, equally spaced hangars, over several square kilometres. The alleys of earth, which separate the buildings, are muddy and strewn with detritus. Here and there, actors wearing full make-up, warm themselves around fires improvised in drums. Heads made of pasteboard; monsters' appendages weaken in the moist fog; paint and make-up streak the puddles, making them iridescent. Rather than going around the warehouses, our guide chooses to walk through them. Most of the hangars are storage areas, not film sets. Rows of wooden boxes, as thick as a forearm, but metres high and wide, are carefully arranged and labelled on either side of the narrow medial path we take. On the ceiling, a gripper slides along two cables, and with two mechanical arms it grasps the selected box, heaves it up and transports it on a small electrical vehicle, which removes it from our sight. All the hangars are identical, and the same warehousing system, the same little electric cars and the same men in orange uniform are to be found in all of them. Impossible to know what the boxes contain, they are all hermetically sealed with planks of wood, and the labelling is in Hindi, Telugu, Chinese and Korean.

It is only after a long walk that the surroundings liven up. First, a scene from a musical comedy from Bombay. Then a chase from Hong Kong, which keeps us transfixed for several long minutes, the time it takes for the bikers to knock down all obstacles. After that there is an embrace from Andhra Pradesh, watched by hundreds of extras with yellow painted faces. There are lots of retakes. Forced to stay still whilst the filming continues and hemmed in by the crowd of extras, who invade the set between scenes, our progression is halted. A wood casing arrives, perched on an electric vehicle. It is carefully placed on the ground, and the men in orange slowly remove the planks, revealing the façade of a temple's pinnacle, chapels, friezes, garlands of smiling faces, petrified figures. I approach: the décor is not of wood or plastic but of visibly old stone. Our guide, a nostalgic smile on his lips, strokes the figure of the peaceful goddess, casts an understanding look at his colleagues, and uses the temporary halt in operations to drag us outside.

As we watch, other elements of décor emerge from their wooden packaging. A mosque, a station, a colonial hotel. All are meticulously realistic; the station's departures and arrivals' board even details the train number. The hotel informs us that it is also one of Cook's Travel agents; a pile of shoes clutters the entrance to the mosque, all different and worn. Each time, our guide stops, looks at them for a long time, sighs, and sets off again. We stick close to his heels, as we are now incapable of finding our own way.

Another shoot, a propaganda film from North Korea, then breaking the alignment of the hangars, in the middle of a clearing, a concrete bunker without any windows. We wait outside, on a sticky bench. Our guide asks our permission to retire, then disappears into the forest. I look at my companions, immobile, seated with equal distance between them, staring straight ahead, their cases on their knees. I get up and I, too, go into the forest. The mist disperses in smoke, the leaves undulate in sheets of metal; the soil dissolves into the earth's surface. Makeshift sheds and folding tables beneath a canvas canopy. This is where the workmen in orange overalls live; some of the backdrops are recognisable, probably stolen from the sets. Salvaged, not stolen. All this belonged to us. How come? We lived in a village which was swallowed up when the dam and lake were built. Once they expropriated us they broke up all the buildings and the ruins are used as background for all the films made here. Beneath the water, the only buildings to remain are hollowed out, blanched. We were relocated here and everyone was offered work in the studios or on the dam. Sometimes we are lucky enough to handle our old school's front window, a piece of our house.

Someone calls me from the clearing; the person we have come to see is ready for us. I catch sight of a small electric car, hand a wad of notes to our guide, slip the case under the seat and set off on a path which leads into the jungle. Later, beneath sonorous foliage, I will use a stone to open the case, from which I will extract sheets of watery light green glazed paper which go with those already in my possession.

26 Our very first clients were enthusiastic about the financial benefits of using **ScriptGenerator©®™**; however, they were apprehensive about how the software actually works, given that it excludes all notion of an author, of ownership and more generally of an 'artist'. Although this anxiety is quite understandable, it is misplaced. All the products developed by our software are matched to an author, the difference being that **ScriptGenerator©®™** treats the author in the same way as all the other elements which make up the contents it delivers: **ScriptGenerator©®™** makes up the author from existing elements and orders its functions within the dictates of the marketplace.

27 It is impossible to overlook the fact that the author is a key element of any commercial strategy. Whether it brands the merchandise ('a book by...', 'a film by...') or is simply a loss leader, the author forms an essential part of the proposed content. Although this is blatantly obvious, it equally has to be acknowledged that at present the industry rarely uses 'artists' to their full potential. In spite of contractual clauses which oblige authors to promote their 'works', in spite of the comprehensive information with which they are supplied prior to any interview, most of them are reticent to engage fully in any marketing operation and, in any event, they are too bland to be of any industrial use. Using the **ScriptGenerator©®™** database, you can produce the author you need to sell the product, and then employ an actor to incarnate this character.

28 **ScriptGenerator©®™** develops the author's life story, personality and the many statements he or she makes, in exactly the same way as any other content it produces. The software draws on its stock of novels, serials, films, true crimes, biographies, profiles and interviews to realise a character who fits the bill, who is used primarily as part of the packaging to showcase the product. He or she is not produced to be a character who reveals all, or who talks politics. **ScriptGenerator©®™** will suggest a number of options, which have been tested and suitably amended so as not to be instantly identifiable. Each one of these solutions can be varied infinitely.

29 The character of the author **ScriptGenerator©®™** produces is not only of particular use for the 'personal memoir' category, which covers documentaries or books of real life experiences, where the author has to be a good fit with the proposed content, but also for the more 'traditional' products, such as audiovisual or written fiction. Thanks to their carefully scripted lives, their issues, their dress codes, their constructed authorial persona, they are ideal and malleable vehicles for your publicity. And, what's more, all their characteristics will be formatted precisely for the appropriate publicity use, be it televised, written or simply iconographic.

30 As was briefly mentioned earlier, producing characters derived from content is obviously not limited to the artists. The lives and roles formatted by **ScriptGenerator©®™** can of course be used for talk-shows, reality TV programs, political forums, newspaper articles – where an icon is always needed – and equally for all sports products. In fact, the lives of footballers, basketball players and boxers influence the consumption of products. Whatever the case, you just need to briefly specify the character types you need, and **ScriptGenerator©®™** will provide them, with all the necessary details filled in.

31 The only differentiation **ScriptGenerator©®™** considers between how authors and characters are treated is that it considers the 'artist' as a never-ending story. Unless you decide to halt the process, **ScriptGenerator©®™** will continue to elaborate on the produced author, specifically linking his itinerary with that of other figures it manages: actors, politicians, etc. As long as photographs are added, the generated material can of course be used immediately – in magazines and television programmes which cover the lives of celebrities.

Refined products

It is never the same day, the same time, but it is always the same airport. I make my way through the journeys which end in shredded notes and the sound of carts rustling on the soil – centimetres of black parallel tracks – right to the taxi queue. Rows of trees, their branches stripped, line the pavement, bent lashes which look as though they stroke the clouds' bellies. The chinks of the city and the outlines of the roads are filled in by a fluid sky. The rectilinear lines traced by the rain are all that is stable on this moving frame: everything shakes, oscillates. Later on, it will be the surge of traffic and reflections from the liquid globules which stream down the car window. Then there will be the familiar television channels, in the hotel, in the room, whilst the evening covers the window with a black paste scaled with luminous rectangles. It will be the start of long hours of fading light.

I read the entire manual on the back of a lorry which drove me out of the jungle (in exchange for my small electrical vehicle). I thought I knew everything there was to know, the aim, the techniques, the project. Then I reread it on the plane. No names or addresses on the glazed pages of paper. Not a single detail; I don't even know if it all exists. Without proof, the manual has no exchange value, even less blackmail value. And from now on I am completely alone, apparently already a wanted man. What's more, I soon realised I was being watched in the cabin, but by whom?

As soon as I turned around, the looks fled like corn beneath the wind. There was a halting exchange, overheard when we disembarked, followed by a series of questions, punctuated by interjections, in the immigration queue, blurred by tannoy announcements. Once through customs, I sat down, clearly visible, on the terrace of a café, so that finally I would be approached. I smiled knowingly to some travellers who seemed to be lingering. I watched the rush-hour come and go, the rhythm of those passing which accelerates until sight fails, bodies that pile up, moving like blocks, the vanishing air. Then the hall emptied out and I had to leave.

In the taxi, in the hotel, the comings and goings, the traffic, continuous flux forms a thick fog. On the surface of this cloudy liquid, pairs of eyes appear, stifling, concentric circles. They immediately dissolve into circular echoes only to reappear further away, beyond. The mass of movement stifles all noise, but ever persistent beneath the row, the sound of continuous whispering can still be heard, irregular steps like stones being shot from a cannon, and the rustling of clothes. In the long corridor which leads to my room, everything becomes more intense. The light forms shadows in the blank panels of the murals, the sound of footsteps coincide with mine and slightly overlap them – if I stop suddenly I can hear those following me – the light beneath the doors is suddenly blocked by attentive shadows. My own breath seems exhaled by someone else, right behind me. All this until the moment the vacuum cleaner conveniently muffles the sound of my pursuers' path. I know contact is imminent, has it perhaps already occurred? In front of the open door, a rectangular metal trolley filled with a bundle of sheets. I jump over the side, slip quickly into this soundless and providential mass, my case close to my stomach. Above, the breathing sounds accelerate and mingle. Then suddenly a slam, words. Promptly, the trolley moves on.

Between the sheets, a rapid procession of neon lights attached to the corridor ceiling, then the bright lights of the utility rooms. The impact against the swing doors, the smell of washing powder and disinfectant. Groups of voices which rise and fall; the sounds of the town when windows are opened. The slow stagnant descent of the lift. Lastly, the machines, dryers snoring, drums banging. The sound of slow progress on the endless conveyor belt of hangers dangling from the rail. A jerky procession of suits, dresses and coats. I will be discovered easily. No, the trolley sets off again, goes down a ramp and suddenly, at ground level, petrol fumes. Raised, and then put into a van. Once the vehicle sets off, I get out of the laundry basket and squat at the end of the trailer.

A long, noisy journey, followed by a decrease in speed, then a stop. I wait; half open the door, no one. I jump out of the van into a vast hangar with tiled walls and very high windows. The rain on the windows forms upside-down fugitive poplars. In the centre, a large heap carefully covered with an oily canvas. On the tip of my finger, I taste the brownish discharge coming from the base; once again it is coltan, several tens of kilos at least, a fortune. Must not get delayed, I head for the small metal door at the far end, crunching on gravel and shards of glass, which echo disproportionately. I have barely turned the handle when the door opens abruptly. Outside, wind and sea, a rectilinear breakwater in the middle, and at the end of the jetty, a motorboat surmounted by the red dot of an incandescent cigarette. He waves to me, I turn around, he calls out to me, I stop in my tracks, he yells my name, has already caught up with me. I have to follow him, board the boat, be quiet, and look at the coast, which quickly fades from sight.

Slowly the purpose of the journey is revealed. Insect legs heaved out of the water, a collection of covered surfaces, hidden areas. The craft's beam of light suddenly reveals the outlines of an object, an oil platform. Or rather a petro-chemical factory out at sea; that's it, a refinery, one can make out the milling sounds coming from the refinery as it cracks the hydrocarbon.

The pillars, dug into the sea, are uniformly smooth; the access ladders removed. Notwithstanding the rolling, I have to grasp hold of the rope-ladder which is thrown out of a hatch high above my head, and climb up slowly, without looking down at the haloes of foam which already suggest my fall. When I reach the top, two strong arms heave me up and guide me onto the slippery surface which is striped with yellow dots, white crosses and red lines, towards the main building. There, I am entitled to a glass of alcohol and a blanket with which to dry off. The installation moans and groans. I wait a long time in this windowless metallic cubbyhole; surely the sun has risen by now?

Finally, a door opens and I go into a room lit by only a rectangular green and yellow Emergency Exit sign, located just in front of me, and above the silhouette of a head which faces me from behind a desk. A chair is offered to me, and then an outstretched hand. I try to shake it, but the fingers snap impatiently, and point to my case. Indecision, I can't part from it just like that. A sound of regular breathing surrounds me. The silence continues and the person on the other side of the desk appears to have turned their back on me. All of a sudden a violent ringing and the neon strips light up. I jump. On mattresses pushed up against the wall, four men dressed in white shirts lift up black masks covering their eyes, yawn, stretch, and look for their glasses. All I can see in front of me is the back of a black leather armchair from which emerge, at mid-height, two bare feet with red-painted toenails, leaning against the partition. One of the men grabs the case whilst the others pin me down. He forces it open, fishes around, ends up finding what he is looking for, and hands over the light watery green glazed paper to the armchair's invisible occupant who, after a while, distributes them to the room's other occupants. The grip gets tighter, I no longer resist.

The process of examining the documents is punctuated by 'we were worried for nothing', 'it's neither here nor there' , 'it's the exact opposite'. But it is not without interest. The details of the room, upon which I have time to dwell whilst they are reading, don't offer any insight, or provide any clues. Pencils on the desk, folders which overflow from beneath the mattresses; alarm clocks which don't show the same time. The sentences I can grasp are no more informative; various languages are combined and the sentences crumble prematurely into murmurs. Once he has completed the manual, the first white shirt allows his hand to linger on his face for a long time, muttering that, after all, he is owed an explanation. The others acquiesce. The black leather chair then turns towards me; its occupant grasps her sandals in one hand and the pages of light watery green glazed paper in the other, stands up and shows me a door.

It is, first and foremost, a huge, sonorous space, steeped in darkness. Once the switch is activated, the shadows throw up a multitude of pipes whose network completely obscures the walls. All the surfaces are covered with a murky layer which is neither frost, nor thick fog, nor smoke, but a sort of vitrified lichen. Swellings and growlings give the impression that the ducts are moving forwards, progressing like paint dripping down a wall. I am at the heart of a refinery in perfect working order, but I can smell neither bitumen nor engine fuel. There aren't any workmen here either; the check points are occupied by great swarms of dust and nothing else. Here, materials less volatile than petrol are separated, but which ones? A bit of everything: ore, cereals, wood, spices. For what purpose? Eliminating raw materials, reducing these basic products to simple ingredients. To show that these layers of primary materials are not irreducible. To spread the predominance of chemistry, to convert materials into formulae. To align the test tubes so that they form spells, and once the sentences are cast, to have available an ear of corn, a pile of carbon, blue traces of cobalt. Never again to have to depend upon this mass of grain and scales, so that finally, once and for all, the blind essence of matter can be obstructed.

We thought that your organisation was working on a similar project, hence your abduction. Have you been following me for a long time? Your partners are very closely watched, yes, we are very frightened of being overtaken by a competing team. You seem to know more about them than I do myself. No doubt, since we have spent a lot of time watching their movements. The machine described in the pages you have just read, where does it operate out of? She scribbles something on the first page of the batch of watery light green glazed paper and hands it to me. None of this matters now; the details of the process which you possess, describes a project which is the exact opposite of which we are striving for. Not to reduce, but, on the contrary, to increase the materials' density, to fill in the grain silos with sentences, to deprive the stories of their references in order that we can make substances which have no origins, Bibles or *One Thousand and One Nights* with starry structures, like minerals or sands. Good luck, you are free to leave.

32 So as not to succumb to advertisers who bombard your company with claims of miracle products, you never invest in a product until you have put the new tool through its paces. We are very aware of the importance of this and extensive trials of **ScriptGenerator©®™** have been planned. However, beforehand, we must explain what forms the contents generated by the software will take.

33 All **ScriptGenerator©®™** products are presented in the form of outlines. Given that the content is intended to be used on a multitude of platforms, the focus is on performative language and only the elements common to all media are spelt out in detail; for example, dialogues, which can be used for film, television and print. All other elements are defined in functional terms: the elements of a décor, a character or a plot, are presented in neutral terms. This type of presentation has been conceived in a way that will not overwhelm you with unnecessary details –always troublesome when you have only a limited time to convince investors, but also to facilitate the production process of audio-visual material and video games in particular. We have chosen to present the content of **ScriptGenerator©®™** to you in the form of a manual. In this way, any sound or image technician will be able to create the product described by closely following the instructions. Once again, this leads to a significant potential reduction in costs.

34 Those entrepreneurs amongst you who are also editors or publishing house directors and, more generally, industrialists of the written word, need to be presented with more than an outline. **ScriptGenerator©®™** is, of course, capable of producing additional elements, but these will always be elaborated from the original outline. In other words, dialogue and events are prioritised over description, which can always be beneficially augmented by photos from newspaper articles and books. Ultimately, you will receive a more dynamic product which is less 'artistic' in content, but much easier to sell precisely because it offers a closer match to products already in the marketplace.

35 Naturally this emphasis on stylistic simplicity serves another purpose: to make easier the translation of all contents, which is crucial to your international game plan. A product which cannot be adapted easily for the five main foreign markets – English, Spanish, Mandarin, Hindi and Arabic – is, of course, destined to fail. Some types of dialogue, such as local dialect and veiled slang, are banished to prevent a surfeit of idioms which would make the product unable to travel. Similarly, the contents of a quest will always rely on a series of universally familiar situations rather than national events. Plotlines will thus carefully avoid offending the sensibilities of consumers in the five major markets, unless a possible ban in one the markets is part of the marketing strategy.

36 Although the process of switching from one language to another needs to be made easy, this does not mean that **ScriptGenerator©®™** systematically eliminates all cultural peculiarities. It is rather that in any given linguistic area, the software prioritises traits which are recognised and appreciated by other cultures, rather than those which would only satisfy the home market. In this way a country or region's most exotic characteristics are pushed to the forefront: local colour, stereotypical behaviour, national dress, etc. – all details which flatter the initial consumers' pride and appeal to the foreign markets.

ScriptGenerator©®™, however, avoids specific political and social problems and any self-referential devices.

37 All these factors governing how the software works do not rule out the production of more complex contents, intended for a more targeted and richer audience. The language protocol **ScriptGenerator©®™** uses can be modified in order to integrate more complex details, such as rhythm, phrasing, effects, figures, and the database further refined so that access to less typical variations can be achieved. These top-of-the-range contents will be presented in greater detail: in addition to the dialogue, **ScriptGenerator©®™** will also write descriptions and situations instead of merely listing the chief characteristics. These out-of-the-ordinary products, even if they originate as films or television programmes, inevitably end up being sold in a printed version. This is because the educated or simply wealthy consumer who buys this type of content needs the gravitas given by the written format, which **ScriptGenerator©®™** can quickly transform into a financial bonanza.

38 More upmarket contents are developed in exactly the same way as the standard ones, with one exception. In order to single out these top-of-the-range products, **ScriptGenerator©®™** combines the language protocols as described in the preceding paragraph according to a recurrent and easily identifiable formula: a formula which will be sold as the content's style. Most importantly, the readers must be able to reproduce this style easily. The top-of-the-range content consumer often enjoys writing in his or her spare time, and the software must provide the user with patterns, in the same way as sewing or knitting magazines do. Our software will take care to ensure that any variation of language inserted into these contents remains easily assimilated, and will periodically insert ironic effects which will flatter the affluent consumer who will only accept being taken in by a knowing wink and a nod, which he will see as a class alliance.

The vastness of the plain gives everything an air of neglect. For kilometres, the soil is flat and striped by even and monochromatic cultivation. Where the farms, silos, hangars, airports or haulage depots have been located can only be explained by random selection and disinterest. If this is not the case, why here and not there? The ever-present dust and the absence of anything which might hinder the wind's progress heighten the impression of everything going to seed. We drive along the roads at an even speed.

When she returned it to me, there was no name on the first page of the parcel of watery light green-coloured paper. Only a longitude and latitude position which I have been trying to locate for some days on this uninterrupted expanse. I have come across virtually no one. One can make out figures on this even horizon easily and early enough to avoid them. Some suddenly emerged from the cultivated land, from the corner of a field, but they had no interest in me.

Planted at regular intervals over the entire area are brushed steel stakes topped with a small polished metal rectangle. They map out gigantic squares so vast they are almost indiscernible to the naked eye. These poles can also be found in the middle of the cultivated land, in a farm yard, in the middle of the parking lot, between two railway tracks. If one follows their alignment over a few kilometres, it turns out that the tenth of a series, be it horizontal or vertical, has a reflective plate on the tip ten times bigger than the others. Initially I thought they charted latitude and longitude, like those plots near Greenwich which indicate the start of the meridian. This was clearly a big error on my part, because, running through these rows of stalks, I did not find what I was looking for.

There is the corpse of a dead cow, half burned to a cinder, across the road. The concrete rail of a hover train covered with graffiti looms up abruptly in a field of rape. A huge pit is full of dark, opaque water; at night it looks as if thin columns of black bubbles rise slowly from the depths without ever bursting. It is impossible to say whether all this is the result of neglect or just a fallow period. In any event, the silence, the lack of spatial organisation, prevents them from being considered as a sign of a past or future catastrophe.

There is definitely some activity, but it is far off, mysterious and agentless. At this distance, one cannot even be sure that the tractor moving forward over there has a driver. The irrigation system operates independently and without warning, as do the silos and beetroot refineries. Although nothing crosses the sun, shadows advance over the plain.

At the end of the track, a car completely blinded by frost. Movement inside. I am all set to turn away when the door opens. A man in overalls emerges, removes a portable stove from the boot and starts to heat a tin of food. I approach, ask for a light, stay to share the meal. On the back seat, two other people huddled in their sleeping bags move their forks silently in white metal lunch boxes. They look as if they belong to a polar expedition, but they are administrators, they are the guardians of the brushed steel stakes. They have been roaming around the area for weeks, checking that the stalks are perfectly straight, that the mirrors are not obscured by soil or bird droppings. After a specified period of time, these administrators are replaced and take up their places in the laboratory.

What do these stakes do? They chart the area under observation. Who does this and from where? A satellite watches over the cultivated land. It is not only growth which is observed but also the appearance of any damaged or parasite-riddled cereals in the middle of the field, where no one ever ventures. The satellite also studies the efficiency of the watering devices, shadings of colour, the famous extraterrestrial circles, those figures drawn by squashing plants with planks, or wild parties. And then there are the illicit activities – farmers mixing maize with poppies. Most important, the regularity of the crop movement, the wind speed which turns them over and the breath of the waves which run through them, the frequency and the height of their oscillations, the presence of currents, hollow areas and crests. All this movement of matter that is imperceptible because flat. The squares, which are delineated by the metal stalks, are visible in photographs because of the mirrors they support, and serve as landmarks.

The administrators' GPS markers pinpoint the area I have been looking for. They lead me to the spot. It is a rectangle of tightly-packed, hard soil, covered with piles of grain dozens of metres high. Neither hangars nor hut. This space appears immutable on the aerial photographs my guides have taken at different times: heaps of cultures have never been moved, their size has remained the same, as has their make-up. The guides set off, leaving me alone. The ground is surprisingly clean, no debris of leaves, no trace of tyres, not even a cigarette butt. I climb a mountain of barley to try to get a better view of the area. Curiously, my legs do not sink in; there is a hard layer beneath the grains. To touch, it is concrete. A building is hidden at the heart of the cereals; I have to find the entrance.

I go past the area in question, probe the soil, and inspect the rows of plantings. In the shadowy light, the ears in the neighbouring fields look like clusters of insects set to fly away in silent clouds, ready to submerge the plain with heavy undulations. One by one I lift up each of the watering hatches, these little cast iron plates which hide the pipes to which the irrigation system is connected. The tenth one is the right one; I unearth a fine metallic ladder. I slide down it.

The well leads to a junction of eight galleries, each of which probably leads to another grain-covered dome. The corridors are empty, lit by neon. Large ducts of electrical wire run along the sides. I choose a direction at random; it has little relevance as I certainly have been spotted. After a few minutes' walk, I end up in a waiting room: green plants, soft music, thick pile carpet, black leather chairs. Copies of the light green watery-coloured glazed paper manual are spread out on a glass table.

39 You will have understood that the purchase of **ScriptGenerator©®™** not only provides you with a tool capable of phenomenally reducing your costs, but it also provides your company with entrance to a very privileged community. Our software gives you access to a multitude of functions which include an exchange made up of content providers, a database which is updated daily, etc. The last, but not least, service we guarantee to provide you with is a team of lobbyists in all major capitals of the world who are at your disposal and responsible for overseeing the interests of all **ScriptGenerator©®™** clients.

40 All users of our software have the same economic profile: they are all transnational communication conglomerates, channels of distribution – the media, audio-visual networks, video game consoles, etc – but also content providers – publishing houses, production houses, advertising agencies, editorial packagers, etc. These similar businesses, though they generate ferocious competition amongst our different clients, share the same legal and political objectives. We have, therefore, formed an entity which is similar to an industrial holding company, even though, for obvious reasons of confidentiality, we have not identified it as such. This entity is managed by lobbyists, part of an extremely focussed network of contacts, who are responsible for developing your interests by influencing both national and transnational governments.

41 If we had to summarise what these interests were in a sentence, it would be: to ensure that groups specialising in the entertainment business benefit from the same advantages as those currently enjoyed by other industries – that is, to limit the constraints imposed on the production and commercialisation of content as much as possible, whilst protecting to the hilt the end product.

42 Open to any suggestions you might have, our team of lobbyists is already focussing on the more important issues. Above all, plagiarism. If we are to consider **ScriptGenerator©®™** as a synthesis of existing content, plagiarism must be defined as loosely as possible so your costs of 'adaptation rights' are kept to a minimum. For instance, the transposition of a known story to a different era should not be considered as plagiarism, but as 'creative reinterpretation'. Similarly, all non-fictions and more generally all 'first person memoirs' should enter the public domain as quickly as possible, and be in no way protected: that you have described a personal experience should not give you any rights over its narration. This loosening of the definition of plagiarism should at the same time go hand in hand with a more rigorous copyright law as it affects new content produced by **ScriptGenerator©®™** client groups. The law must protect products which dominate the current market, and take all the rest as support products.

43 The second issue deals with the establishment of privacy rights over the products of the entertainment industry. You should soon be entitled to benefit from the same advantages enjoyed by agribusinesses and heavy industries, the power to effectively patent the processes and recipes used in the making of your products (see paragraph 5). Making public the existence of our software should entail sanctions as punitive as those applicable to someone who reveals the recipe of a fizzy drink, a convenience food, or even the plans of an aeroplane engine.

44 The third issue concerns the removal of the final obstacles to further concentration in the entertainment industry. Our most recent success stories include the repeal in the United States of the law forbidding television networks to take over other channels which can be watched by more than 35 per cent of the population, as well as the quashing of the rules preventing a company from having control over a television station, a press group and a cable TV operator that cover the same local audience. Next, we will go for EU anti-trust laws.

45 Our fourth and last priority is to facilitate the emergence of an effective ruling class in the entertainment industry. All the great industrial revolutions have occurred thanks to a homogeneous class, and obviously your sector is no exception.

It is interesting to note that in television, film and publishing, the strategic managerial positions in the industry are increasingly held by members of the same families, and directors' children – be they producers, actors or filmmakers – increasingly marrying amongst themselves. The integration of this social class has to be speeded up, and this can be done by, on the one hand, facilitating the inheritance of capital from parents to children and, on the other, by making it more difficult for members of other social classes to enter the industry.

Art

Sliding glass doors divide the rooms. Scaled-down shapes, both familiar and out of focus, emerge from a series of mirror reflections. Amidst this compression of moving and frosted images, the anonymous décors through which one has passed thousands of times are all there to be seen: office floors, hotel halls, luxury boutiques, stations and airports. These monotonous and open spaces are uniform like grey beaches.

The doors open and close automatically, with the sound of muffled metal. There are many rooms, most empty. It is impossible to get the measure of the place. Nobody; just automated humming sounds hard to locate. One slides along the surface of an all-glass building, whose every window reflects parts of the neighbouring buildings. The corridor grid finally fans out to give onto an oval room in the middle of which stands a long table with twenty computers on it. Changing shapes unfurl on the screens, none of which seems to bear any relation to each other, although they all seem to be animated by a mute unity. Waves of words pass from one machine to the next, lists scroll from left and right, from top to bottom, like spirals of smoke, bubbling sentences which ooze along the glass.

Everything goes much too fast, it is impossible to read what comes up on the screens. At a guess, something is being organised, units incorporate themselves in what must be a canvas, an almost empty frame which, each time it reappears, darkens. Each undulating mass billows on the computer screens like a school of fish and displays a unique texture, starred, stratified, compressed. Some crumble like sand, others adhere together.

No doubt the products described in the manual are made here. The activity seems constant, and yet without the usual features of industry. Nothing but silent work, imperceptible insect movements. Active subterranean rivers, leeching out. The words arrange themselves in procession, weave teeming networks, then stick together, forming swarms which are then forwarded to the client. In vain I search for printing machinery in the neighbouring spaces, but nothing. Everything is achieved at a distance, by a secure link.

I continue to venture forth, end up in another concrete corridor, which must lead to another vaulted room hidden beneath a mound of culture. There, dozens of metallic clamps handle newspapers, books, cassettes. Televisions, loudspeakers broadcast a heady rumbling sound, as they fast forward through a series of documents. Each machine is linked up to a computer, which transcribes all the scanned contents. This is where the database is enriched. At the far end, a blaze of flashes, photographs, magazines and volumes, one page and sheet at a time. The green light of the scanners, the uninterrupted rustling of pages turning. The crystal-clear glacier-like transparency of the glass structures. This endless stream of memories electronically frozen. These cracklings one thinks one hears, followed by abrupt, loud thrusts.

Why is there no dust here? Who controls these machines, these consoles? I try to call out but no sound comes from my throat, as if it were very cold. It suddenly becomes harder to move forward, the atmosphere seems to rarefy, and the space becomes opaque. I give up the idea of exploring the other rooms; in any event, I already know what they hide. There will be the costume bank, where clothes are scanned from every angle; the décor room, which contains real props, old stones, pieces of archways, finely carved doors. I have to go back to the first room, the one in which the products are made. My limbs are numb; the silence hangs over me like a frost.

The raw materials still feature on the first screens. Then packets streaked with soot and twigs come to a standstill, to form domes. The letters of the alphabet – insects caught in the radiation's amber light. And all the while, crackling sounds. My whole body is stiff, and I can feel a slow but formidable pressure in my back. The walls and furniture leave the ground and as they move imperceptibly they tilt in blocks rent by the vibration of the assembly line, as if iced over by a glacier river. I now realise I should have explored the other rooms, where I most certainly would have discovered men and buildings already caught by the mirrors, dislocated by the flows and the fractures. The space around me is hard and crevassed, my legs squeezed into transparent flanges, my head immobilised in a frozen lock.

Rumblings would have to be generated in the middle of this cold trap which, in years to come, would work on the glacier until it exploded. Using my free hand, I randomly tap the keyboard which lies within my reach, in an attempt to stir up monsters and spectres impacted in the matter.

So many shadows race before my eyes, wide with frost.

46 To give you an idea of what our software is capable, **ScriptGenerator©®™** has produced the story which features in between the chapters of this manual. You will notice that it adheres to the basic formula described earlier: there is an investigator – the narrator, a sought-after object – the manual which you are holding, and relevant events. The three elements are well balanced because the investigator is absolutely banal, whereas the object of his quest and the obstacles he comes up against are much less so. The range of raw materials, from which our software has drawn technical details, elements of vocabulary, actors and plot, is one of the key elements of the seeming originality of the product.

47 Of course, the content has been assembled from pre-existing components, mostly from true stories. Similarly, all the secondary characters have been sourced from newspaper articles (the intermediary is a well-known diamond trafficker, and the men carrying the suitcases are members of a group who have masterminded several financial scandals which have recently been discovered in Europe). Equally, all the locations exist (the Swiss hotel is in Davos, the film studios in the Indian state of Andhra Pradesh, and the Central African diamond mine is twenty kilometres north of Bouar). **ScriptGenerator©®™** sourced all descriptions from the press. Our software has used specialist publications in raw materials: these include the *Cyclope™ Annual* (Editions Economica, France), different directories (*Mineral Yearbook™*, *Mineral Commodity Summary™*) newsletters from Indigo Publications™ (Paris), as well as despatches from the Bridge

News™, Reuters Commodities™ and Dow Jones Commodities™ agencies. If you join the **ScriptGenerator©®™** user club we would be happy to supply you with a complete list of the references used to produce the content you have just read.